THE
DRAGONSITTER
DISASTERS

The Dragonsitter first published by Andersen Press in 2012
The Dragonsitter Takes Off first published by
Andersen Press in 2013
The Dragonsitter's Castle first published by
Andersen Press in 2013

This bind-up edition first published in 2014 by
Andersen Press Limited
20 Vauxhall Bridge Road
London SW1V 2SA
www.andersenpress.co.uk

4 6 8 10 9 7 5

British Library Cataloguing in Publication Data available.

ISBN 978 1 78344 122 8

Printed and bound in Great Britain by CPI Group (UK) Ltd,
Croydon CR0 4YY

THE DRAGONSITTER DISASTERS

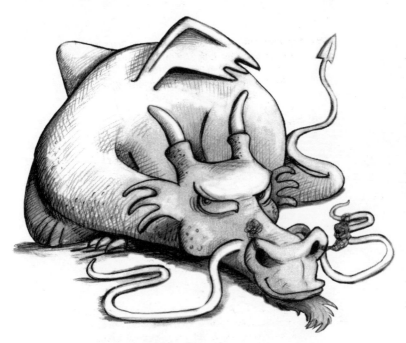

Josh Lacey

Illustrated by Garry Parsons

Andersen Press
London

Contents

The Dragonsitter

From: Edward Smith-Pickle

To: Morton Pickle

Date: Sunday 31 July

Subject: URGENT!!!!!!!!

Attachments: The dragon

Dear Uncle Morton,

You'd better get on a plane right now and come back here. Your dragon has eaten Jemima.

Emily loved that rabbit!

I know what you're thinking, Uncle Morton. We promised to look after your dragon for a whole week. I know we did. But you never said he would be like this.

Emily's in her bedroom now, crying so loudly the whole street must be able to hear.

Your dragon's sitting on the sofa, licking his claws, looking very pleased with himself.

3

If you don't come and collect him, Mum is going to phone the zoo. She says she doesn't know what else to do.

I don't want the dragon to live behind bars. I bet you don't, either. But I can't stop Mum. So please come and fetch him.

I'd better go now. I can smell burning.

Eddie

Dear Uncle Morton,

I'm sorry for getting so cross when I wrote to you earlier, but your dragon really is quite irritating.

I hope you haven't changed your flight. If you have, you can change it back again. I have persuaded Mum to give your dragon another chance.

Luckily she didn't see him chasing Mrs Kapelski's cats out of the garden.

Uncle M, I do wish you'd told us a bit more about your dragon. You just handed him over and said he'd be fine and got back in your taxi to go to the airport. You didn't even tell us his name. And some instructions would have been helpful.

Mum and I don't know anything about dragons. Emily says she does, but she's lying. She's only five and she doesn't know anything about anything.

For instance, what does he eat?

We looked for help on the internet, but there was nothing useful.

One site said dragons only eat coal. Another said they prefer damsels in distress.

When I told Mum, she said, "Then I'd better look out, hadn't I?"

But your dragon doesn't seem so fussy. He eats just about anything. Rabbits, of course. And cold spaghetti. And sardines and baked beans and olives and apples and whatever else we offer him.

Mum went to the supermarket yesterday, but she's got to go again today. Usually one shop lasts us a whole week.

Also, you could have warned us about his poo. It smells awful! Mum says even little puppies are trained to go to the loo outside, and this dragon looks quite old, so why is he pooing on the carpet in her bedroom?

But I can see why you like him. When he's being sweet, he really is very sweet. He has a nice expression, doesn't he? And I like the funny snoring noise he makes when he's asleep.

Are you having a lovely time on the beach? Is the sun shining? Are you doing lots of swimming?

It's raining here.

Love from

your favourite nephew,

Eddie

PS. The smell of burning was the curtains. I put out the fire with a saucepan full of water. Luckily it had dried by the time Mum saw them.

Dear Uncle Morton,

I wish I could say things were better with the dragon today, but actually they're worse. This morning, we came downstairs for breakfast and found he'd made a hole in the door of the fridge.

I don't know why he couldn't just open it like everyone else. He drank all the milk and ate yesterday's leftover cauliflower cheese.

Mum was furious. I had to beg her and beg her and beg her to give him one more chance.

"I've already given him one last chance," she said. "Why should I give him another?"

I promised to help clear up any more of his mess. I think that was what changed her mind.

I'm hoping he'll go in the garden from now on.

Mum is keeping a bill for you. It's now two supermarket shops and a new fridge. She says she'll charge you for the carpet too if she can't get the stains out.

I sent you two emails yesterday. Didn't you get either of them?

Eddie

From: Edward Smith-Pickle
To: Morton Pickle
Date: Monday 1 August
Subject: Your dragon again

📎 **Attachments:** Poo close-up

You might have to change your flights after all, Uncle M. Your dragon's done another poo in the house. This time, he couldn't get into Mum's room, because she's been keeping her door shut, so he did it on the landing right outside. I scrubbed it with bleach, but there's still a stain on the carpet. I just hope Mum won't see it. If she does, she'll ring the zoo right away, I know she will.

E

From: Edward Smith-Pickle

To: Morton Pickle

Date: Tuesday 2 August

Subject: Tethers

 Attachments: Me putting out fire

Dear Uncle Morton,

What's a tether?

I don't know and Mum won't tell me, but she's at the end of hers.

That's what she says, anyway.

It was the curtains that did it.

Mum saw them last night. She was furious, but I managed to calm her down. I said I'd pay for new ones out of my pocket money.

I don't actually have any pocket money, but I promised to start saving immediately.

Also I pointed out that the hole was really quite small.

Mum gave a big sigh, shrugged her shoulders and stood on a chair and turned the curtains round so you could hardly see the hole. Not unless you were looking for it, anyway. And why would anyone get down on the floor and search for holes at the edge of the curtain?

Then, this morning, the dragon breathed all over them again.

It was really quite dramatic. The whole room filled with smoke. While I was running backwards and forward with a saucepan full of water (six times!), your dragon just sat on the sofa. I wasn't expecting an apology, but he could at least have looked embarrassed.

Also, he knows he's not allowed on the sofa.

This is my fifth email to you, Uncle M, and you haven't replied to one of them. I know you're on holiday but, even so, could you reply ASAP. Even if you can't come and collect your dragon, some tips on looking after him would be v much appreciated!

Edward

PS. If you don't know what ASAP means, it means As Soon As Possible.

PPS. Your bill is now: 3 supermarket shops, 2 curtains, 1 fridge, 1 rabbit, 1 new carpet. (Mum saw the stain.)

Dear Uncle Morton,

Mum rang your hotel. They said you never arrived. They said you cancelled your reservation and they gave your room to someone else.

So where are you?

Mum says you've been lying to us. She says you've always told lies, even when you were a boy, and she was stupid to think you might have changed.

I didn't know what to say, Uncle Morton. I was sure you hadn't lied to us. I don't believe you're a liar. But if you're not staying at the Hotel Splendide, why did you give us their number? Where *are* you staying?

I told Mum anything might have happened. Maybe you banged your head and you don't know who you are. Maybe you're in hospital, covered in bandages, and no one knows who to call. Maybe you've been kidnapped. You're always talking about your enemies. Do you need us to pay a ransom? I hope not, because your bill with Mum is already quite enormous.

Mum doesn't think you've been kidnapped.
Or bumped your head. She says you're
just a selfish pig and always have been,
and once you've collected your dragon she
never wants to see you again.

I'm sure she didn't mean it, Uncle M.

Little sisters are always saying stuff like
that. Emily does too. The next day, she's
forgotten what she even said.

Mum's probably just the same.

But even so, I think you should call her
ASAP.

Eddie

From: Edward Smith-Pickle

To: Morton Pickle

Date: Tuesday 2 August

Subject: The zoo

Dear Uncle Morton,

Mum is about to ring the zoo. She's going to ask them to take the dragon away.

I tried to persuade her not to. But she said it was the dragon or her.

I said the zoo probably wouldn't want her.

She said I should be careful because I was treading on thin ice.

I don't know what she meant, but I didn't want to ask. She had that expression on her face. Do you know the one I mean? The one that says: "you'd better keep out of my way."

So I have.

E

From: Edward Smith–Pickle

To: Morton Pickle

Date: Tuesday 2 August

Subject: Don't worry!

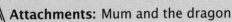
Attachments: Mum and the dragon

Dear Uncle Morton,

The zoo aren't coming. They thought Mum was joking.

When they realised she was serious, they thought she was crazy.

Finally they put the phone down.

So she rang the RSPCA, but they didn't believe her, either.

They said, "There's no such thing as dragons."

Mum said, "Come here if you want to see one."

That was when they put the phone down too.

Now Mum doesn't know what to do. She's threatening to kick the dragon out in the street.

I said she couldn't just leave a poor defenceless dragon out in the middle of the road where anything might happen to him.

"I've got to do something," she said. "Or I really will go crazy. What if he bites the neighbours? What if he eats one of the twins?"

It's true, he could easily pull them out of their pram. They live opposite and they're only eight months old. With teeth like his, he could gobble them up in a moment. I know you said he'd never harm another living creature, but that wasn't true, was it? What about Jemima?

Uncle M, I must have written you ten messages by now. Could you please write back?

Eddie

Dear Uncle Morton,

You're not going to believe what's happened now. The dragon just attacked Mrs Kapelski's cats again. This time the garden is full of fur, and the petunias have gone up in smoke.

It was their own fault, I suppose, because they know they're not allowed in our garden. They came in anyway. They always do. They didn't see your dragon snoozing on the patio. They were rolling around on the grass when he woke up and jumped on them.

Tigger got away without any problem, but the dragon managed to grab Maud's tail in his jaws.

I saw it all through the French windows. I was banging on the glass, trying to make the dragon stop, but he took no notice.

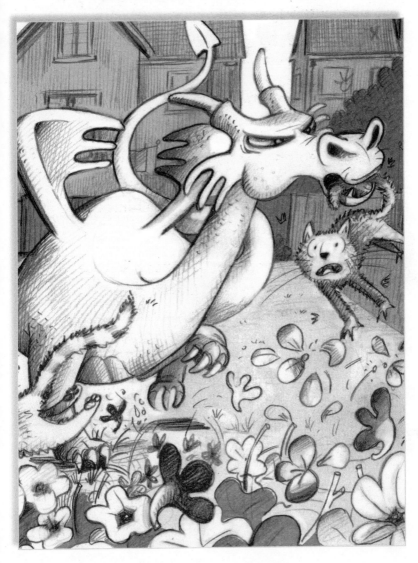

Finally Maud turned round and scratched him on the nose. The dragon wasn't expecting that! He was so surprised, he opened his jaws and she was over the fence in a second. He breathed a great burst of flame after her.

Luckily he missed.

Unluckily he got Mum's petunias.

Luckily Mum didn't see what happened. She was on the phone to the pet shop. She's been ringing everyone she can think of, but no one wants a dragon.

Now she's sitting at the kitchen table with her head in her hands. She's run out of people to ring. I haven't told her about the petunias yet, but she's going to see them soon, and then I don't know what will happen.

To be honest, Uncle M, I'm a bit worried about her. I asked about mending the fridge and she said, "What's the point? The dragon will just make another hole in it."

I suppose she's right, but even so, it would be good to have somewhere to keep the milk.

Eddie

PS. You'll be glad to hear Maud is fine. She's still got all her tail.

PPS. Your dragon has spent the rest of the morning picking fur out of his teeth. He won't be attacking any more cats in a hurry.

Dear Uncle Morton,

I don't even know why I'm writing to you. You haven't answered any of my other emails. Maybe I've even got the wrong address, just like Mum's got the wrong hotel. But I've got to tell someone what's happening and I can't think of anyone else to tell.

Today was the worst day so far. Your dragon set fire to the postman.

To be fair to the dragon, I don't think he meant to. I think he must have been frightened by the letters coming through the letterbox. He breathed fire all over them. The flames went through the letterbox and out the other side, setting the postman's sleeve alight.

28

Luckily the postman wasn't hurt. Mum
put the flames out with a blanket. But he's
going to need a new uniform and he said
he'll charge us for it.

We had a lot of explaining to do. There was a big fire engine parked outside the house and four firemen in our front garden, wanting to check our smoke alarms.

Mum told them about the dragon. She invited them in to see him.

The firemen looked at one another in a funny way and backed down the garden path.

When they'd gone, the postman said he'd sue us. He said he'd report us to the police. He said we could expect never to get another letter in our lives. He said a lot more things which I didn't actually hear because Mum put her hands over my ears.

Now Mum's upstairs in bed. She said she'll come downstairs to make supper, but I don't know if she really will.

The dragon is lying on the sofa. I told him he should be ashamed of himself, but he doesn't look ashamed at all.

He won't get off the sofa, either. Not even when I shout at him. He knows quite well he's not allowed on there.

Eddie

Dear Uncle M

I've just been through the remains of our letters and found a postcard with a foreign stamp. Unfortunately there was nothing else left, just the corner with the stamp on, but I think the picture might have been of a beach. Did you send it to us? If you did, that's very nice of you, but it would be even nicer if you would answer my emails.

E

From: Edward Smith-Pickle

To: Morton Pickle

Date: Friday 5 August

Subject: Our tummies are empty

Attachments: The dragon in the kitchen

Dear Uncle Morton,

I am quite a long way past the end of my tether.

Yesterday I didn't think things could get any worse, but they just have.

Mum is upstairs again. She says she's not getting up till the dragon's gone. I said that might not be for three more days and she said, "Then I'm going to be spending a lot of time in bed. You'd better find me some good books."

Emily and I haven't had any breakfast and it looks as if we're not going to get any lunch, either.

Your dragon is in the kitchen. The door's shut.

He won't let me in. I just tried, but he breathed a little trickle of flame in my direction. From the expression in his eyes, I could see it was a warning.

I'm not a coward, Uncle M, but I'm not stupid, either. I ran straight out and slammed the door behind me.

I waited for a few minutes, then I peered through the keyhole and saw what he'd done.

He's been through the cupboards, smashing down the doors and tearing out all the food. He's ripped open the packets. He's chewed through the tins. There's rice and lentils and spaghetti hoops all over the kitchen floor.

Uncle Morton, what am I supposed to do?

Edward

From: Morton Pickle
To: Edward Smith-Pickle
Date: Friday 5 August
Subject: Chocolate

Have you tried chocolate?

What do you mean, have I tried chocolate?

Of course I have! I love chocolate.

I don't want to be rude, Uncle Morton, but I'm beginning to worry Mum might be right about you. I've been sending you emails for almost a whole week now and I've been begging you to answer and when you finally do, you just ask if I've ever tried chocolate.

Maybe you really have banged your head!

Have you?

If you haven't, then why haven't you answered any of my other emails? Where have you been? And when are you going to come and collect your dragon?

Edward

I mean, have you tried giving the dragon chocolate?

It works!!!!!!!!!!!!!!

Attachments: Our very own flame-thrower

Dear Uncle Morton,

I'm sorry I haven't replied more quickly to tell you what happened, but I've been too busy feeding the dragon all the chocolate in the house and then going to the shop to get some more.

The dragon is a changed beast.

Mum says he's been behaving like a little angel and he has. He's stopped stealing food. He poos on the grass. He doesn't even sit on the sofa any more. Actually that's not quite true, but he gets off as soon as he's told to.

Tonight we had a barbecue in the garden. Your dragon lit it.

Then he ate six sausages, three chops and nine baked bananas. Luckily Mum had just been to the supermarket, so there was enough for us too.

Now your dragon is lying on the floor, looking at me with his big eyes. I know I shouldn't give him any more chocolate. I don't want him to get fat. But I'm just going to give him one more piece and then it's time for bed.

Eddie

Dear Uncle Morton,

I thought you might like to know your dragon has now eaten:

12 bars of milk chocolate

14 bars of plain chocolate

6 Twixes

1 Crunchie

and 23 bags of Maltesers.

The man in the shop is starting to look at me in a funny way.

I thought Mum would mind buying so much, but she said, "If he's happy, I'm happy."

He is. Very.

Even Emily has forgiven him. She seems to have forgotten all about Jemima. I think she'd like to have your dragon as a pet instead.

She's started calling him Cupcake.

I've told her several times that Cupcake isn't a suitable name for a dragon, but she takes no notice.

Does he actually have a name?

If he doesn't, I would suggest Desolation. Or Firebreath. Or something like that.

But not Cupcake.

I hope you're enjoying the last few hours of your holiday and managing to get a last swim and some sunshine. It's raining here.

See you tomorrow. Don't miss your flight!

Love from

Eddie

From: Morton Pickle

To: Edward Smith-Pickle

Date: Saturday 6 August

Subject: Re: Re: Re: Re: Re: Re: Chocolate

Attachments: My island; Hotel Bellevue; Les Fruits de Mer d'Alphonse

Hi Eddie,

Very glad to hear that my tip about chocolate did the trick. It always does with dragons, even the biggest of them. I remember hiking through the mountains of Outer Mongolia with a rucksack almost entirely stuffed with Cadbury's Fruit & Nut. Without it, I wouldn't be here today. I fed the whole lot to the biggest dragon I've ever seen in my life, a bad-tempered chap with teeth as big as my hands and terrible breath.

I'll tell you the whole story when I see you, but I don't have time now. I've got to be quick. I'm in the airport and my flight leaves any minute. But I wanted to write to you and say I AM SO VERY SORRY for not reading your messages earlier in the week. I could have checked my mail at the hotel, but I had resolved not to interrupt my holiday. That was stupid of me, I know, and I am exceedingly apologetic. I only looked yesterday because I had heard a rumour from a fellow guest that there have been terrible floods in Lower Bisket, the town opposite my island. I have several good friends living there, so I wanted to check they were safe. (You'll be glad to know that the floods were actually in Upper Buckett, which is quite different.)

I'm very sorry too that my naughty little dragon has been behaving himself so badly. Were my instructions no use at all? I was quite sure I had included the tip about chocolate.

Will you please apologise to your mother about the mix up over hotels? I had been planning to stay in the Hotel Splendide, which is why your mother had their address and phone number. On arrival, I discovered that their chef, the famous Alphonse Mulberry, had quarreled with the owner and moved to an establishment in the next town along the coast. So I moved there too. I'm glad I did. His cooking is even more spectacular than I had remembered.

For some reason I don't appear to have your mother's email address, which is why I'm sending this to you. Please apologise to her on my behalf. I have bought her an enormous chunk of Roquefort as a present. I know how much she likes cheese.

They're calling my flight. I'd better go and join the scrum. I'll see you very soon.

Lots of love from your affectionate and apologetic uncle,

Morton

Dear Uncle Morton,

I hope you had a good journey home. Did the dragon behave himself on the train?

Mum put up the new curtains and she's ordered another fridge from the shop. She says she never liked the petunias and she's decided to plant roses instead. She's going to spend the rest of your money on a new carpet for all our bedrooms.

She loves the cheese, by the way.

I don't. It smells awful. Sorry for saying so, but it does.

Emily says "thank you" for the monkey. She says he's almost as good as Jemima. I think he's even better. At least he doesn't need feeding. Also he can sleep in her bed instead of that cage at the end of the garden.

And thanks very much for the books. They'll be really useful if I ever learn French.

You know your list of instructions? Well, Mum finally found them down the back of the sofa. We've read them now. You did say the thing about chocolate, and lots of other useful stuff too. If only we'd found them before!

Mum says she thinks you just put them down there when you came to collect the dragon, but I told her not to be so silly.

Mrs Kapelski's cats have started coming into the garden again. Mum chased them out with a hose. She said, "I wish that dragon was still here." Then she looked at me very quickly and said, "I don't really."

But I think she does.

I do too.

He made everything very difficult, but he was fun too.

I hope you're having a lovely time back home on your island.

By the way, when I said I'd like to come and visit, I really did mean it.

Will you send an official invitation to Mum? Otherwise she's never going to let me.

Emily would like to come too, but I told her she's too young. She is, isn't she? She might fall off a cliff or something.

Lots of love from

your favourite nephew,

Eddie

PS. Please give Ziggy a Malteser from me.

The
Dragonsitter
Takes Off

Dear Uncle Morton,

I know you don't want to be disturbed, but I have to tell you some very bad news.

Ziggy has disappeared.

Mum says he was asleep on the carpet when she went to bed, but this morning he was nowhere to be seen.

I'm really sorry, Uncle Morton. We've only been looking after him for one night, and he's run away already.

He must hate being here.

Actually he did seem depressed when you dropped him off. I bought him a box of Maltesers as a present, but he didn't eat a single one.

I've been reading your notes. There's lots of useful information about meal times and clipping his claws, but nothing about what to do if he disappears.

Should we be searching for him, Uncle Morton? If so, where?

Eddie

Dear Uncle Morton,

We're back from school and Ziggy still isn't here.

While we were walking home, Emily said she saw him having beans on toast in the café.

I was already running to fetch him when she yelled, "Just joking!"

I don't know why she thinks she's funny, because she's really not.

Mum rang Mr McDougall. He said he would row to your island first thing tomorrow morning and look for Ziggy. He can't go now because there's a storm.

I'll let you know as soon as we hear from him.

Eddie

From: Edward Smith-Pickle

To: Morton Pickle

Date: Monday 17 October

Subject: READ THIS FIRST!

 Attachments: Cupboard

Dear Uncle Morton,

Don't worry about my other two emails. We have found Ziggy.

He was in the linen cupboard. I suppose he'd crawled in there because it's nice and warm.

Mum was actually the one who found him. You would have thought she'd be pleased, but in fact she was furious. She said she didn't want a dirty dragon messing up her clean sheets. She grabbed him by the nose and tried to pull him out. He didn't like that at all. Luckily Mum moved fast or he would have burnt her hand off.

I think she's going to charge you for repainting the wall. There's a big brown patch where he scorched the paint.

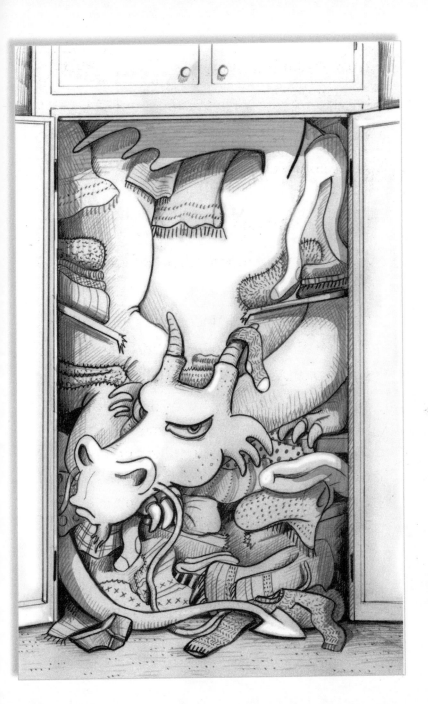

I still think he might be depressed.

We had macaroni cheese for supper. I saved some for Ziggy and left it outside the linen cupboard. When I checked just now, he hadn't even touched it.

But at least he's here and not wandering the streets.

Love from

Eddie

Dear Uncle Morton,

I just wanted to tell you nothing has changed.

Ziggy won't move from the linen cupboard.

He still hasn't eaten a thing. Not even a Malteser.

I'm really quite worried about him.

To be honest, I'm also a bit annoyed, because I had been planning to take him to school today.

When I told Miss Brackenbury why I hadn't brought anything for Show and Tell, she just laughed and said I could do it next week instead.

I hope Ziggy will have come out of the cupboard by then.

Eddie

From: Morton Pickle

To: Edward Smith-Pickle

Date: Wednesday 19 October

Subject: Re: Ziggy

Attachments: The ashram

Hi Eddie,

Sorry I haven't replied before, but we're forbidden from using any electronic devices at the retreat. I have sneaked down to the village to read my mail.

Please tell your mother that I'm very sorry about her linen and will, of course, buy her a new set of everything. And don't worry about Ziggy's appetite: if he gets hungry, he will eat.

Thanks again for looking after him. I would never have been able to come here otherwise.

The retreat is exhausting and strangely wonderful. We are woken at five o'clock in the morning and spend four hours sitting in silence before breakfast. The rest of the day is devoted to yoga, pausing only for a meal of vegetable curry and rice. My mind is clear and my body contorts into shapes that would have been impossible only last week.

Love from your affectionate uncle

Morton

Dear Uncle Morton,

Are you sure Ziggy is a boy?

I think he might be a girl.

I mean, I think she might be a girl.

You're probably wondering why I'm thinking this, and the answer is very simple.

She has laid an egg in the linen cupboard.

Now I understand why she likes being in there. Not only is it nice and warm, but she's built herself a nest from Mum's clean sheets and towels.

The egg is green and shiny and about the size of a bike helmet.

71

Do you think I could take it to school next week for Show and Tell?

I promise I won't drop it.

Ziggy still isn't eating. Mum says she was ravenous when she was pregnant with me and Emily, but maybe dragons are different.

Eddie

Dear Uncle Morton,

There is a tiny crack in the egg. I'm sure it wasn't there yesterday.

Mum says I have to go to school, but I don't want to. What if the baby comes when I'm not here?

She's calling me. I've got to go.

It's so unfair!

If you get this, please, please, please will you ring Mum and tell her someone needs to stay with the egg?

E

Dear Uncle Morton,

I'm glad to say the baby hasn't arrived yet.

When Mum picked us up and brought us home, I went straight upstairs to the linen cupboard.

The egg was still there.

It has changed, though. It's covered in more cracks.

Also it keeps shaking and shuddering as if something is stirring under the surface.

I'm not going to sleep tonight.

Eddie

From: Edward Smith-Pickle

To: Morton Pickle

Date: Saturday 22 October

Subject: It's here

Attachments: His first step; Birthday boy

Dear Uncle Morton,

This is the most amazing day of my life.
I have just watched a baby dragon being
born.

I didn't stay up last night. Mum made me
and Emily go to bed.

I tried to sneak out of my room, but she
heard me and sent me back.

Then I tried to stay awake in my bed, but I
must have drifted off, because when I next
opened my eyes, it was 6.43.

I got out of bed and tiptoed down the
corridor to the linen cupboard. I thought I
would have missed everything, but there
was the egg, still in one piece.

It had changed again, though. It was covered in hundreds of little cracks.

I must have stood there for at least half an hour, watching and waiting, but nothing happened.

I was just about to go downstairs and grab some breakfast when the shell cracked open and a leg popped out.

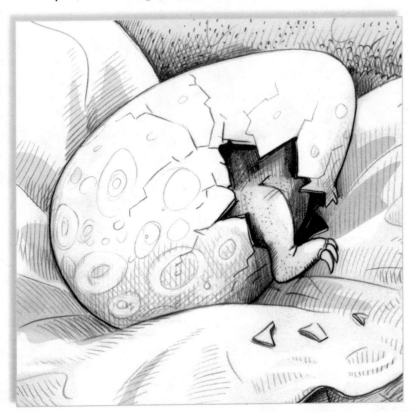

I stayed absolutely still. I don't think I even breathed.

The little green leg wiggled and waggled. I could see the four miniature claws stretching and flexing as if they were trying to find something to hold on to.

I thought Ziggy might get involved, but she just sat there, watching.

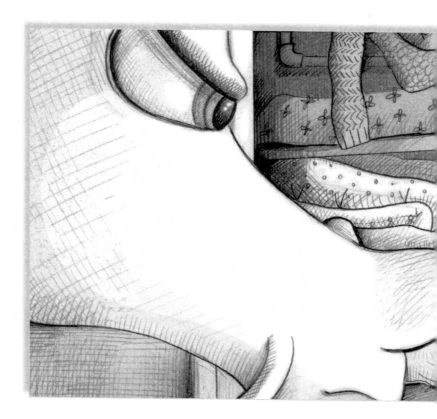

Suddenly more shell shattered and another leg popped out.

Then a bit of a body. And a head.

There it was.

A baby dragon about the size of a small pigeon.

It pulled itself out of the egg and rolled onto the pillowcase, leaving a trail of broken shell.

If I had picked it up (which I didn't) it would have fitted in the palm of my hand.

That was when Ziggy finally seemed to notice her baby. She leaned over and started licking it.

I ran downstairs and grabbed some food from the fridge. Ziggy is still refusing to eat, but the baby seems to be hungry. So far it's drunk a bowl of milk and eaten two cold potatoes and half a sausage.

I wanted to give it some chocolate as a treat, but I don't know if sweets are good for babies.

I wish you were here to see it.

Love from

Eddie

Hi Eddie,

I was overjoyed to get your email and the beautiful pictures. What wonderful news! I'm delighted, and not a little envious. One of my greatest ambitions has always been to witness the birth of a dragon.

I also feel very stupid. It had never occurred to me that Ziggy might be female. I could have checked, I suppose, but I know a man who lost three fingers doing that, so I'd never tried.

Which reminds me: don't touch the baby!
It might bite.

I have discussed my circumstances with
Swami Ticklemore and he recommended
that I did not stop the retreat early. Would
you mind taking care of Ziggy and her child
for a few more days? I should be able to
leave, as planned, at the end of the week.

Morton

From: Edward Smith–Pickle

To: Morton Pickle

Date: Sunday 23 October

Subject: Arthur

Attachments: Happy baby

Dear Uncle Morton,

You don't have to worry about the baby biting. He's very friendly and sweet. All he does is play and eat and sleep.

He poos too, but they're very small, so I don't mind clearing them up.

Emily says he's the cutest thing she's ever seen.

I have called him Arthur. I hope you like the name. If you would prefer something else, please let me know ASAP.

Obviously I don't actually know if he's a boy or a girl, and I'm not going to try and find out, but he looks very boyish to me.

If he ever lays an egg, could you change his name to Gwendoline? That was Emily's choice, and I promised she could have it if he turned out to be a she.

Right now he is snuggling up with Ziggy in the linen cupboard. Mum is cooking a big spaghetti bolognese for all of us to have for supper, dragons included.

Love from

Eddie

From: Edward Smith-Pickle

To: Morton Pickle

Date: Monday 24 October

Subject: Help!

Attachments: Him; Mum fights back

Dear Uncle Morton,

You've got to help us. There's a massive dragon in our garden and he won't go away.

He arrived just before bedtime. Mum was running the bath when we heard a terrible bang.

Mum thought the roof had collapsed. I was worried an asteroid had crashed into the house.

We ran outside to have a look.

The first thing we saw was the TV aerial lying in the middle of the garden.

About twenty tiles from the roof had fallen down there too.

Then we saw why.

An enormous dragon was sitting on our house. Smoke was trickling out of his nostrils, and his tail was flicking from side to side, knocking more tiles off the roof.

Ziggy must have heard the noise too, because she came outside to see what was going on.

As soon as she saw the dragon, she breathed a huge burst of flames in his direction. I thought it was her way of saying hello, but I soon realised she was telling him to get lost.

It didn't work. The big dragon flew down and charged towards her, gushing flames from his nostrils as if he was planning to roast her alive.

Ziggy sprinted back into the house, pushing Arthur in front of her.

The big dragon actually tried to follow us inside, but Mum chased him out again.

She bashed him on the nose with a broom.

I said she should be careful, but Mum said she wasn't scared of some silly dragon, however fierce he might look.

She just rang you seven times. I said you weren't listening to your messages, but she kept leaving them anyway.

If you get this, please call us ASAP.

Eddie

From: Edward Smith-Pickle

To: Morton Pickle

Date: Monday 24 October

Subject: Goodbye????

 Attachments: I hope he's not hungry

Dear Uncle Morton,

The big dragon is still here. He's lying on the patio, watching us through the windows, as if he's waiting for the perfect moment to smash through the glass and come inside.

He has scary eyes.

Do you think he could be Arthur's dad?
Is that why he's here? Has he come to see
his son?

But why won't Ziggy let him?

Can dragons get divorced?

Mum says I have to go to bed now.

If you don't get any more messages from
me, it's because I've been eaten by a
massive dragon.

Eddie

Dear Uncle Morton,

We're all still here. Including the dragon. He spent the night in the garden. There's not much left of Mum's plants.

I think he's been trying to talk to Ziggy. He's certainly been breathing a lot of fire in her direction and making some strange barking noises.

She must be able to hear him, but she pretends not to. She's just been lying in the kitchen with her head in Mum's lap.

I don't know why they're suddenly such good friends.

When I asked Mum, she said "Female solidarity".

I've got to go to school now. I'm taking Arthur for Show and Tell. He's coming with me in a shoebox. I hope Miss Brackenbury likes him.

Love from

Eddie

From: Edward Smith–Pickle

To: Morton Pickle

Date: Tuesday 25 October

Subject: Stuck

 Attachments: No exit

Dear Uncle Morton,

It's me again.

We couldn't leave the house. The big dragon blocked our way.

Mum told him to step aside, but he took no notice.

They stared at one another for a long time.

You know how fierce Mum can be, but the dragon didn't even blink.

One of them had to move first and it turned out to be the dragon.

He breathed a sizzling jet of flame in our direction.

Mum shoved me and Emily back inside,
then slammed the front door.

We tried to sneak out twice more, but he
was always waiting for us.

So we can't go to school, which is cool.

Maybe this big dragon isn't so bad,
after all.

Eddie

From: Edward Smith-Pickle

To: Morton Pickle

Date: Tuesday 25 October

Subject: Sums

Dear Uncle Morton,

I was wrong. Staying at home is even worse than going to school. Mum made us do sums all morning. She's going to make us do more this afternoon.

Luckily I've got an idea for how to get out of here.

I remembered what you said about once taming a massive dragon in Outer Mongolia with a rucksack full of chocolate.

I'm going to try the same trick with this one.

Wish me luck!

Eddie

Dear Uncle Morton,

It didn't work.

Mum saw me heading for the front door with an armful of sweets and confiscated the lot.

Now she and Ziggy are sitting on the sofa, watching telly and sharing a box of Maltesers.

I told Mum she was eating our only chance of escape, but she just laughed.

I think we're going to be stuck in here for ever.

Eddie

Dear Uncle Morton,

I know you're not supposed to talk till Friday, but *please* could you call us?

Today is even worse than yesterday.

The dragons have been fighting all morning. The big one broke down the back door and rampaged through the house. He knocked over the telly and broke our kitchen table in half. Also he's knocked almost all the pictures off the wall.

We had to lock ourselves in the loo.

We finally came out when the house was quiet.

Ziggy had chased the big dragon into the garden. I don't know how she did it.

She and Arthur are lying on what's left of the sofa. Every single cushion has been burst open. There are feathers everywhere.

Emily is very upset because we've got nowhere to sit.

I'm more worried about what the big dragon will do next.

Mum just rang the retreat and spoke to Swami Ticklemore. He said you couldn't be disturbed.

Mum said it was an emergency, but Swami Ticklemore wouldn't change his mind.

If you get this, please call Mum ASAP.

Eddie

From: Morton Pickle
To: Edward Smith-Pickle
Date: Wednesday 26 October
Subject: Re: Please call us!
Attachments: Meditation

Hi Eddie,

I'm very sorry, but I can't leave the retreat early. Swami Ticklemore says I would do permanent damage to my inner peace.

I shall hurry out of here at dawn on Friday and come straight to your house.

I don't know exactly why the big dragon is bothering you, but I should imagine he is no different to any other proud father and simply wants to meet his son. Maybe you should let them spend some time together?

If that's not possible, why don't the three of you go and stay in a hotel?

You can tell your mother that I will, of course, pay for the room.

M

Dear Uncle Morton,

Mum didn't like your idea about staying in a hotel.

She looked at me as if I was a complete idiot. Then she spent about fifteen minutes saying why oh why was she surrounded by such stupid, selfish men.

I think she means you, Dad and the dragon.

She might have meant me too. I'm not sure.

Anyway, Uncle Morton, couldn't you talk to Swami Ticklemore again and ask for special permission to leave early?

Otherwise you might have to pay for more than a night in a hotel.

If the dragons carry on like this, you'll have to buy us a new house.

Eddie

From: Edward Smith–Pickle
To: Morton Pickle
Date: Wednesday 26 October
Subject: Flying

Attachments: Up; Up; And away!

Dear Uncle Morton,

You won't believe what just happened.

I was in the sitting room with Arthur and Ziggy when the big dragon appeared at the window. He started breathing fire and making those strange barky noises.

Obviously I don't know what he was saying, but I could see Ziggy listening to him. Then she seemed to be talking to him. Finally she went to the door.

She looked at me. I knew what she wanted. I undid the latch. The three of us walked outside – Ziggy first, then Arthur, and finally me.

The big dragon started flapping his wings, slowly at first, then faster and faster.

Arthur hopped onto his back.

They lifted into the air.

I thought this was the last time I would see them. I wished Mum and Emily had been there to say goodbye. Then I turned to look at Ziggy and saw she was lowering her neck down to the ground.

There was a strange expression in her eyes.

I realised it was an invitation.

I'm so glad Mum and Emily were upstairs, because if they'd been watching, they would have screamed at me to come back inside.

But I was alone. So I could do what I wanted.

I lifted my leg over Ziggy's neck and clambered onto her back. As soon as I was settled, her wings flapped and we went up – past the trees – and up – above the roofs – and up, and up and up and up and up and up.

I was flying!

I knew I shouldn't look down, but I couldn't stop myself. The garden was already tiny.

I could see the other dragon above us, his huge body silhouetted against the sky.

Higher and higher we went. Till we were
swallowed by the clouds. I couldn't see
anything except whiteness. It was really
chilly too. If Ziggy hadn't been so warm,
I would have been frozen solid.

Suddenly we broke through the top of the clouds and we were in sunshine. The big dragon was just ahead of us. With a few flaps of her wings, Ziggy was alongside him.

I could see Arthur hopping around on his dad's back, but I held on as tightly as I could, wrapping my arms around Ziggy's neck. I didn't have wings to save me if I slipped off.

Suddenly the big dragon flipped over. Then up again.

Ziggy did it too.

For a moment I was upside down!

Next they both looped the loop.

Three times.

It was like being in the Red Arrows.

Up and down we went. Round and round. The two dragons taking turns to do tricks as if they were saying to each other, *Look at me! Can you do this too?*

I thought I might be sick, but actually it was Arthur who was.

I suppose he is only four days old.

The others must have thought he'd had enough then, because suddenly we were diving down again, heading for the ground.

We were going so fast, I thought we'd crash through the house. But at the last moment, the two dragons pulled back and we landed gently on the patio.

The three of them are dozing now, but I wanted to come inside and tell you all about it.

Eddie

From: Edward Smith–Pickle

To: Morton Pickle

Date: Wednesday 26 October

Subject: He's gone

📎 **Attachments:** Quiet time

Dear Uncle Morton,

Don't worry about leaving the retreat early. You can stay as long as you like. That big dragon has gone and I don't think he's coming back.

Mum says he probably has another girlfriend somewhere, and maybe he does, but I'm sure that's not really why he's left.

I think he came here to see his son, and now he has, so he can go.

Taking Arthur into the air must have been his way of saying goodbye.

I suppose it's the same as Dad taking me to the cinema before he drives back to Cardiff.

Everything is very peaceful here now it's just the five of us.

Mum and Ziggy are watching a black and white movie on telly.

Arthur and Emily are playing Monopoly. Neither of them know the rules. They're just pushing the pieces around the board and making a mess of the money. Emily keeps giggling and Arthur is blowing little spurts of smoke through his nostrils.

I hope you enjoy your last day at the retreat, and see you on Friday.

Eddie

From: Morton Pickle

To: Edward Smith–Pickle

Date: Saturday 29 October

Subject: Re: He's gone

 Attachments: Home sweet home; Clipping

Hi Eddie,

We are finally home after an interminable train journey and a stormy ride in Mr McDougall's boat. The house feels much smaller with two dragons, even if one of them is only a baby. When Arthur grows up, I'll have to build him and Ziggy a home of their own.

I want to thank you again for looking after them so well.

Please tell your mother that I really am very sorry about all the trouble that they caused.

You probably won't like me saying so, but I do think she was right about Arthur. Having a pet is a serious responsibility.

If I were you, I would accept her offer. I know gerbils aren't exactly exciting, but you can always get something bigger when you're older.

Will you please also tell your mother that I was entirely serious about the retreat. I could see how stressed she is. Nothing would make her feel better than a week of silence and yoga.

While she is with Swami Ticklemore, you and Emily could stay with me. I know Ziggy and Arthur would love to see you – as would I.

Lots of love from your affectionate uncle

Morton

PS Did you see this?

Saturday 29th October

The Scotsman

IS IT A BIRD?
IS IT A PLANE?
NO, IT'S A DRAGON!

Photograph courtesy of Annabel Birkinstock

Passengers on a British Airways flight to Paris were treated to an extraordinary spectacle when two enormous green creatures flew past their plane.

Neither the pilot nor air traffic controllers noticed anything unusual, but at least a hundred passengers are convinced that they were visited by dragons.

Fashion consultant Annabel Birkinstock could hardly believe her eyes. She flies from London to Paris at

Fashion consultant Annabel Birkinstock

least once a month, and has seen everything from David Beckham to the Eiffel Tower, but she was astonished when she looked out of the window and spotted a dragon flying past.

"At first I thought it might be a huge bird," said the shocked twenty-seven-year-old. "But I've never heard of birds breathing smoke from their nostrils."

Aviation expert Graham Tulse has examined photographs taken by passengers on the plane and said the "dragons" were probably just an illusion caused by sunlight and cloud cover.

"The stewards must have been serving too many free drinks," he scoffed. "One of the passengers even claimed there was a boy riding on a dragon's back!"

Annabel Birkinstock doesn't agree. "I know what I saw," she told us last night. "Those weren't rainbows or shadows. They were undoubtedly dragons."

The
Dragonsitter's
Castle

From: Edward Smith-Pickle

To: Morton Pickle

Date: Monday 26 December

Subject: Look who's here

📎 **Attachments:** Unexpected guests

Dear Uncle Morton

I just tried calling you, but the phone made a funny noise. Have you changed your number?

I wanted to tell you your dragons are here.

They must have arrived in the middle of the night. When I came down for breakfast, Ziggy was sitting on the patio, peering through the window, looking very sorry for herself.

I didn't even see baby Arthur. I thought Ziggy had left him at home. Then I realised he was tucked under her tummy, trying to keep warm.

They're feeling better now we've given them some toast and let them sit by the radiator.

Have they come to say Happy Christmas?
Are you coming too? I'm afraid we haven't
got you a present, but there's lots of turkey
left and about a million brussels sprouts.

Love from

Eddie

From: Edward Smith–Pickle

To: Morton Pickle

Date: Tuesday 27 December

Subject: Collection

Dear Uncle Morton

Your dragons are still here. They have eaten the entire contents of the fridge and most of the tins in the cupboard too.

Arthur also swallowed three spoons and the remote control.

Mum says they will probably come out the other end, but I'm not really looking forward to that.

She wants to know when you are coming to collect the dragons.

We're leaving first thing on Thursday morning, so she says could you get here by Wednesday afternoon at the latest?

Eddie

From: Edward Smith-Pickle

To: Morton Pickle

Date: Wednesday 28 December

Subject: Please call us!

Dear Uncle Morton

Your phone is still making the same noise. Mum says you've probably been cut off because you haven't paid your bill.

Does that mean you haven't got my emails either?

So what are we supposed to do with the dragons?

We're leaving first thing tomorrow morning.

Mum has to catch the 9.03 or she won't arrive in time for the meet-and-greet with Swami Ticklemore.

She is going on that yoga retreat like you suggested. She says she deserves it after the year she's had.

I asked if the dragons could stay here without us, but she said no way, José, which you have to admit is fair enough after last time.

Emily and I are going to stay with Dad in his new house. He says it's a castle, but Dad's always saying things like that.

I rang him and asked if we could bring the dragons.

He said no, because his new girlfriend Bronwen is allergic to fur.

I told him dragons don't have fur, but he said even so.

So please come and get them ASAP.

Eddie

PS I've been waiting with my rubber gloves, but there's still no sign of those spoons or the remote control.

From: Edward Smith-Pickle
To: Morton Pickle
Date: Thursday 29 December
Subject: Where are you????

Dear Uncle Morton

Mum says if you're not here in the next ten minutes, she'll leave the dragons in the street and they can take care of themselves.

I said you couldn't possibly get from Scotland to here in ten minutes, and she said worse things happen at sea.

I have literally no idea what she meant.

Now she and Dad are shouting at one another just like they used to when they were still married.

If you get this in the next ten minutes, please call us!

Eddie

From: Edward Smith-Pickle

To: Morton Pickle

Date: Thursday 29 December

Subject: Don't go to our house!

Attachments: Car; castle

Dear Uncle Morton

I hope you haven't left already to pick up the dragons, because they're not at our house any more.

Dad said they could come to his castle after all.

I don't know what changed his mind, but he did say the Welsh have always had a soft spot for dragons.

Luckily Bronwen had stayed behind, so there was room for all five of us in the car.

Dad was worried about his seats, but I told him dragons can be very careful with their claws if they want to, and I'm glad to say they were.

We got a lot of strange looks on the
motorway, and there was a nasty moment
when Arthur flapped his wings and almost
got sucked out of the window, but now
we've arrived at Dad's new castle, and we're
all fine.

It really is a castle!

There's a moat and half a drawbridge and a rusty old cannon by the front door.

Dad bought it cheap because the previous owner had lost all his money.

He is going to convert it into apartments and sell them off and finally make his millions.

Our bedroom is in a turret. There's a little wooden staircase which goes to the top and you can see for miles.

The only problem is it's freezing. Dad says that's the price you have to pay for living in a historical building, but I don't see why he couldn't just buy some heaters.

Here is the address:

Manawydan Castle,
Llefelys,
Near Llandrindod Wells,
Powys, Wales

Dad says please come and pick up the dragons ASAP because he and Bronwen are having a party on New Year's Eve and they want everything to go perfectly.

Eddie

Dear Uncle Morton

I forgot to say: please bring some medicine
for Ziggy.

She's got a terrible cold.

When she sneezes, little jets of fire
come out of her nostrils. I hope it's not
contagious.

Eddie

From: Morton Pickle

To: Edward Smith-Pickle

Date: Thursday 29 December

Subject: Re: Flu

📎 **Attachments:** Snow; McDougall to the rescue

Hi Eddie

I'm very sorry that I haven't replied before, but my communication with the outside world has been severed for more than a week by the thick layer of snow smothering my island. I even had to dig a path from my back door to the shed so I could bring back some dry logs for the fire.

My boat was frozen solid, so I couldn't possibly get to the mainland, and I spent the festive season alone, reading several excellent books and eating my way through whatever I could find at the back of my cupboard. Luckily I had stocked up on my last trip to France, so I spent a very happy Christmas eating duck paté and drinking some wonderful red wine.

The dragons weren't so content. They huddled by the fire for the first couple of days, then disappeared. How very sensible of them to come and find you.

I polished off the last of my tins last night and raised a red flag. Luckily Mr McDougall saw it first thing this morning and came to rescue me in his boat.

I'm now checking my emails in his house. He sends Season's Greetings, by the way, and hopes to meet you soon.

I'm sorry to hear that Ziggy is unwell. Please try to keep her and Arthur comfortable until I arrive. I wouldn't want them to fly any further south. They'd only get lost.

Mr McDougall's nephew Gordon is giving me a lift to the train station. I have just checked the timetables. If I make my connections at Glasgow and Crewe, I should be with you tonight.

With lots of love from your affectionate uncle

Morton

From: Edward Smith-Pickle

To: Morton Pickle

Date: Friday 30 December

Subject: Champagne

Attachments: Snowdragon

Dear Uncle Morton

We're all very glad you're coming!

We're going out now to pick up the drinks for the party, but we'll be back by six o'clock.

If you get here early, Dad says the pub in the village is excellent, although he advises against the pickled eggs.

Bronwen says please don't bring any more snow, because we've got enough already. It came down last night and we're now knee-deep.

We just went out to make a snowman, but we made something much better instead. Here's a picture. Can you guess what it is?

Arthur jumped around all over the place, making funny little barking noises, then challenged the snowdragon to a duel.

He melted a hole in its middle, which made him even more confused.

If the snow hasn't gone in the morning, will you help us make another?

Eddie

From: Edward Smith-Pickle
To: Morton Pickle
Date: Friday 30 December
Subject: Medicine

Attachments: Hottie

Dear Uncle Morton

I'm really sorry. Arthur has caught his mum's cold.

It's my fault. I shouldn't have let him play in the snow.

I've given them hot water bottles, but they won't stop sneezing.

I hope you're bringing lots of medicine.

Eddie

From: Edward Smith-Pickle

To: Morton Pickle

Date: Friday 30 December

Subject: When you get here

Attachments: Rockets

Dear Uncle Morton

We're going to bed now, but Dad will leave the door unlocked. We've made up a bed for you on the sofa in the sitting room, which is actually the warmest room in the castle.

I asked if you could stay for the party, but Dad said only without the dragons, so I suppose that means no.

I wish you could. It really is going to be a great party.

We've been helping Bronwen make the canapés. There's smoked salmon and mini pizzas and cheese straws and chicken wings, plus enough crisps to fill twelve huge bowls.

Bronwen wants us to take everyone's coats when they arrive. Dad has bought about a million fireworks to set off at midnight.

Dad says we can stay up to watch. I reminded him that Emily is only five, but he said it would be good for her.

I said Mum would be furious, and he said she'd be furious whatever he did, which is probably true.

Eddie

Dear Uncle Morton

Are you stuck in a snowdrift?

I hope not, because Dad is going to evict the dragons if you're not here by lunchtime.

I said he can't make sick dragons sleep outside in this weather, and he said hard cheese.

Eddie

From: Morton Pickle

To: Edward Smith-Pickle

Date: Saturday 31 December

Subject: Re: Cheese

Attachments: McDougall to the rescue again

Sorry about delay. Helping McD rescue sheep from unexpected avalanche.

Gordon taking me to station now.

With you 4pm at latest.

M

From: Edward Smith–Pickle

To: Morton Pickle

Date: Saturday 31 December

Subject: Canapés

 Attachments: Crime scene

Dear Uncle Morton

Could you try to get here before 4pm?
The dragons have ruined the party, so
we have to leave the castle right now.

It happened when we came back from
making the second snowdragon. I was
just taking off my boots when I heard
a terrible scream. I thought Emily must
have seen another mouse. I ran into
the kitchen and found a scene of total
devastation.

There were vol-au-vents everywhere.
The floor was covered with crisps.
Somehow twenty miniature Scotch eggs
had got stuck to the ceiling. The entire
platter of smoked salmon had gone,

including all six lemons and the pepper grinder.

Bronwen said she'd only nipped outside for a second to fetch another jar of mayonnaise, but she must have been gone for longer than that, because not even Ziggy can eat 600 canapés in one second.

I thought the dragons might at least look guilty, but I've never seen anyone looking so pleased with themselves.

The good thing is they must be getting better if they're hungry.

I didn't say that to Dad, because I could see he wasn't in the mood.

When Bronwen finally stopped shouting,
she said in a quiet voice, enough is enough,
and it was them or her.

Dad said he was sorry, but he hardly knew
the dragons, and they were big enough to
look after themselves, and then he said
some things about you, Uncle Morton,
which you probably don't want to know.

I said if the dragons left then I was leaving
too.

Emily said so was she.

Dad told us not to be ridiculous, but we
weren't.

You'll find us at the castle gates.

I hope you'll be here soon, Uncle Morton,
because the forecast is more snow.

Eddie

Dear Uncle Morton

You'll be glad to hear we're back in the castle. It's not much warmer than outside, but at least we don't get covered in snow.

Dad came to get us. He made a deal with Bronwen. She doesn't mind the dragons staying if they're locked in our turret at the top of the castle. We have to stay with them till you arrive.

See you at 4pm if not before.

Eddie

Dear Uncle Morton

It's 8.20 and the first guests have just arrived.

We're still stuck in the turret with your dragons.

I said what about the coats, and Bronwen said the coats could take care of themselves.

Where are you?

E

Hi Eddie

I'm sure you're safely tucked up in bed at this unearthly hour of the morning, but I wanted to wish you a very Happy New Year.

I'm terribly sorry that I haven't reached you yet, but the avalanche turned out to be more serious than first thought, and I've been helping Mr McDougall retrieve a hundred and eleven sheep that had been scattered around the hills.

They are all now safely in his barn. We have just celebrated midnight with a chorus of Auld Lang Syne and a magnificent single malt whisky that the McDougalls had been saving for a special occasion.

Gordon will give me a lift to the station first thing. I should be with you in time for tea.

Morton

From: Edward Smith-Pickle

To: Morton Pickle

Date: Sunday 1 January

Subject: New address

Attachments: The big bang; night flight

Dear Uncle Morton

I'm very glad to hear you're finally coming to Wales, but please don't go to the castle. We're not there any more. We are staying in the Manawydan Arms in Llefelys.

You're probably wondering why we're not staying in the castle, and the reason is very simple. Ziggy burnt it down.

You can't exactly blame her (although Dad does) because she didn't mean to.

It happened last night. The four of us were in the turret, looking out of the window, watching cars pulling up and guests hurrying into the castle.

I now know you were four hundred miles

away, Uncle M, but I didn't at the time, and I kept hoping to see you.

Emily and I had our duvets, but the dragons were freezing. There was snow coming through the holes in the windows. I was worried the two poor shivering dragons would get pneumonia.

Then I had a great idea. Our room had a fireplace. Why didn't we use it?

I sneaked downstairs and grabbed some wood and a newspaper. Dad had taught me how to scrunch up the paper and make a pyramid from the kindling. He did tell me never to light a fire without adult supervision, but we were so cold I had to do something. I was just looking round for some matches when Ziggy sneezed and the whole pile burst into flames.

For a moment we were lovely and warm.

Then a rocket whooshed past my left ear and exploded against the ceiling.

Someone must have left a box of fireworks in the kindling basket. Maybe I picked some up by mistake when I was gathering wood. They do look very like ordinary sticks.

Another rocket shot across the room and through the window, smashing the one

pane of glass that wasn't already broken.

A Catherine Wheel span across the floor and down the stairs.

One of the fireworks must have set fire to a curtain or a duvet, and suddenly the turret was in flames.

Emily screamed so loudly I thought my eardrums might burst. I was trying to stay calm, but I was beginning to panic too. It was extremely hot and quite difficult to breathe, and our route downstairs was blocked by a thick wall of black smoke.

There was only one way out.

We had to go up.

We charged to the top of the turret, followed by the dragons. Fireworks were exploding in every direction. Down on the ground, I could see guests flooding out of the castle.

We screamed for help, but no one could hear us.

Luckily Ziggy knew what to do. She bent her neck and flapped her wings.

All three of us hopped aboard.

When we took off, there was a huge cheer from all Dad's guests. They must have thought we were part of the display.

I had expected Ziggy to land beside Dad, but she flew into the woods and landed under a big tree.

Once she was on the ground, she refused to move. She and Arthur just curled up in the snow. I said it wasn't a sensible place for a snooze if you've got a cold, but they took no notice.

Emily and I had to walk home. We were both shivering. Emily's lips turned blue.

Just when I thought we might die of frostbite, I heard someone shouting our names. I shouted back. It was Dad. He came running through the trees and gathered us both up in his arms and said he'd thought we were dead. I'd never seen him cry before.

The fire had died down by the time we got back to the castle. Dad gave the firemen a crate of champagne to say thank you. The labels had burnt off the bottles, but they didn't mind.

Emily and I are sharing a room in the Manawydan Arms. Dad is asleep next door. He's probably going to kill me when he wakes up.

I wish I could say Happy New Year, but it really isn't.

Eddie

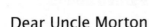

Dear Uncle Morton

I don't know where you are or what's happened you, but if you do ever get here, we are still staying at the Manawydan Arms. It's the only pub in the village and Dad says you can't miss it.

The three of us went back to the castle today. There's not much left, just a few blackened walls and some smouldering timbers.

In case you're wondering why there are only three of us, Bronwen has gone to her mother's in Aberystwyth. She and Dad had a big row last night.

Bronwen said sorry to me and Emily for her

language, but I said she shouldn't worry, we'd heard it all before when Mum and Dad were getting divorced, and worse too.

Bronwen said Dad obviously hadn't learned from his mistakes, and he said she was right about that. That was when she left.

There's still no sign of the dragons. Dad says they're old enough to look after themselves, but Arthur certainly isn't, and I'm not sure if Ziggy is either, especially when she's got a cold.

Also Dad says I owe him a new castle.

I thought he was joking, but he's not.

Apparently he borrowed all the money to buy the castle, and now he'll never be able to pay it back.

He's ruined, and it's my fault.

Today is only the second of January, but this is already turning out to be the worst year of my life.

Eddie

Dear Uncle Morton

I'm a terrible dragonsitter. There's still no sign of Ziggy or Arthur, and I have no idea where they might be.

There's no sign of Bronwen either, but Dad said not to worry about her, because there are lots more fish in the sea.

Emily said he could get married to Mum again, but Dad said he'd been married to her once already and that was enough for any man.

Dad is going back to the castle today. Emily and I are going with him, and we'll search the forest for your dragons.

Eddie

From: Morton Pickle

To: Edward Smith-Pickle

Date: Wednesday 4 January

Subject: Re: Lost

Attachments: Lower Biskett church

Dear Eddie

I'm terribly sorry to hear about the castle. Please pass on my apologies to your father. I don't have the funds to pay for a new castle, but I will help in any way that I can.

I'm sorry that I haven't reached you yet, but there has been a crisis in the village. The weight of snow on the church roof caused it to collapse. Mr McDougall and I, along with all other able-bodied men and women, have been called upon to help.

You will be glad to hear we have now repaired the worst of the damage. I'm going to the station now and shall be with you this afternoon.

Don't worry about Ziggy and Arthur. I have read that the caves of North Wales were once full of dragons, so they have probably sniffed out some distant relatives. We shall search for them together when I arrive.

Morton

From: Edward Smith–Pickle
To: Morton Pickle
Date: Wednesday 4 January
Subject: Quiz Night

Dear Uncle Morton

We have reserved a room for you at the Manawydan Arms.

It's Quiz Night tonight and there's a prize of a hundred pounds, which would be really useful now I'm saving up to buy a new castle.

If you get here in time, you could join our team. I bet you're brilliant at quizzes.

We spent today at the castle again, but there's still no sign of your dragons. I hope you're right about them hiding in a cave. I'm just worried they won't be warm enough.

Eddie

From: Morton Pickle
To: Edward Smith–Pickle
Date: Thursday 5 January
Subject: Re: Quiz Night

Delayed again. Leaving now.

Sorry to miss quiz.

M

Dear Uncle Morton

The Manawydan Arms is full. They won't reserve a room for you, because you didn't use the one they kept for you yesterday, but you can sleep on the floor in ours.

Dad is driving us home first thing tomorrow morning, so you can keep the room if you want to stay here while you search for the dragons.

Don't worry about missing Quiz Night. We came second and won a prize of fifty pounds!

When I told Dad I would add it to his savings for a new castle, he told me not to be ridiculous and bought a round of drinks for everyone in the pub.

173

I suppose that's what Mum means about him being useless with money.

He had a piece of good news yesterday, so there was something to celebrate. The man from the insurance company thinks his policy should pay out in full because the fire was caused by misadventure and/or faulty equipment.

Emily told him that the fire was actually caused by a dragon trying to keep warm.

The insurance man said he'd never heard that one before.

Dad gave me a look, so I kept quiet, and we pretended Emily has a vivid imagination.

See you later.

Eddie

From: Morton Pickle

To: Edward Smith-Pickle

Date: Friday 6 January

Subject: Re: Our last night

📎 **Attachments:** Home sweet home

Dear Eddie

I hope you're safely home by now. I'm terribly sorry that I never reached Wales and didn't get a chance to see your father's castle. However, it all turns out to have been for the best.

I was finally ready to catch a train yesterday when I remembered that you had asked me to bring some medicine. I have a large stock in my bathroom cabinet, so I borrowed Mr McDougall's boat and whizzed across the channel to my island.

I moored the boat and hurried up the path to the house, and was just reaching for my keys when who should I see lounging on the lawn. . .

There they were, my two dragons, enjoying this morning's unexpected sunshine. They showed no shame for causing so much trouble. All they wanted was a snack and a belly-rub, and happily I was able to provide both.

You'll be glad to hear that their coughs and colds are entirely cured. I'm sorry they didn't behave themselves, but thanks again for looking after them so well.

Perhaps this year you will finally come and visit us?

Love from

Morton, Ziggy and Arthur

Dear Uncle Morton

I'm very pleased the dragons are safe. I was getting quite worried they might never be found.

We're home too and everything is fine.

Mum says THANK YOU for recommending the ashram. (She asked me to put that in capital letters.) She says she's never felt so relaxed in her entire life.

It's true. She didn't even mind about the burn marks on our pyjamas.

She wants to go back ASAP, so maybe I could come and stay then?

Happy New Year!

And lots of love

from your favourite nephew

Eddie

PS Will you keep looking in Arthur's poos? Mum says the spoons don't matter, but it would be good if we could turn on the telly.

Instructions for dragonsitting

As you know, Ziggy has an excellent appetite and will happily snack all day long, but I try to restrict his mealtimes to the same as mine.

He will eat anything except curry and porridge.

Please don't give him ice cream. It plays havoc with his digestion. He does love it, though, so don't leave any within reach.

Don't forget: dragons will do anything for chocolate! I usually keep several bars of Cadbury's Fruit and Nut for emergencies.

Ziggy isn't an energetic creature. He usually sleeps all night and most of the day, and requires only a little gentle exercise. If he's feeling restless, he'll take himself for a quick flight and be home in time for tea.

I usually let him outside to do his business after breakfast and before bedtime. Accidents will happen and I shall, of course, recompense you for any damage.

He is perfectly happy curling up anywhere, even the hardest cold stone floor, but will be grateful for a couple of cushions. Please don't let him sleep in your bed – I don't want him getting into bad habits.

I have clipped his claws, so you shouldn't need to. If you do, I recommend garden shears.

If his rash recurs, call Isobel Macintyre, our vet in Lower Biskett. See other sheet for number. She knows Ziggy well and could help in a crisis.

If you have a non-medical emergency, try Mr McDougall. I'll leave you the number for the ashram, but it will probably go unanswered. As the swami says, "Silence is the sound of inner peace."

Thanks again for looking after Ziggy and see you on Friday.

M

From: Morton Pickle

To: Alice Brackenbury

Date: Tuesday 8 November

Subject: Re: School visit

Dear Miss Brackenbury,

Thank you so much for your delightful email. There was no need to introduce yourself; Eddie has told me how much he enjoys your lessons, which, I can assure you, is a great compliment from my nephew.

I'm touched and flattered by your suggestion that I should visit the school and give a talk about my travels. I have indeed been to some extraordinary places, and I always enjoy chatting about the months that I spent tagging penguins in Patagonia or my voyage in a leaky canoe down the furthest tributaries of the Amazon.

However, I chose some years ago to come and live on a small island, just off the coast of Scotland, and I have many duties here. I am also, I must confess, a nervous public speaker, and your students would probably be bored by my ramblings.

Instead of myself, may I offer a copy of my book? It will be published by a small press next year – the title is: The Winged Serpents of Zavkhan: In Search of the Dragons of Outer Mongolia.

I shall send a couple of copies to Eddie and ask him to bring one to school. You might like to read a few pages to your class. Obviously I wouldn't want to encourage schoolchildren to hunt for dragons – they are quiet creatures and prefer to be left alone – but I should like to inspire the younger generation with a respect for wildlife and a longing for adventure.

With all best wishes

Morton

The Dragonsitter's Island

Josh Lacey
Illustrated by Garry Parsons

Dear Uncle Morton,
The McDougalls are here. Mr McDougall won't stop
shouting and waving his arms. He has lost three sheep
in a week. Now he wants to take your dragons away
and lock them in his barn till the police arrive.

Eddie is dragonsitting on
Uncle Morton's Scottish island.
But something is eating the
local sheep. Can Eddie find
the real culprit?

Praise for *The Dragonsitter*:
'Short, sharp and funny'
Telegraph

9781783440450 £4.99